JOHNNY
RIDES AGAIN

JOHNNY RIDES AGAIN

JO ANN MUCHMORE

Holiday House/New York

Copyright ©1995 by Jo Ann Muchmore
ALL RIGHTS RESERVED
Printed in the United States of America
FIRST EDITION

Library of Congress Cataloging-in-Publication Data
Muchmore, Jo Ann.
Johnny rides again / Jo Ann Muchmore.—1st ed.
p.   cm.
Summary: After their mother and their old dog die within months of
each other, ten-year-old Rose and her brothers have to make some
adjustments when they get a new dog and their father begins to date.
ISBN 0-8234-1156-7
[1. Dogs—Fiction.   2. Family life—Fiction.   3. Remarriage—
Fiction.]   I. Title.
PZ7.M8697Jo   1995   94-19466   CIP   AC
[Fic]—dc20

For Les and Monte

JOHNNY
RIDES AGAIN

Chapter 1

"**L**ook! Here comes one!" Harry hollered. "He's picked *us* out!" Sure enough, that little blue heeler puppy was trying to run across the straw, tumbling and sliding and yipping, as fast as he could, straight to Harry and Luke.

I was leaning up against the shed wall, so disgusted I thought I might gag. You couldn't on earth get *me* in on this dopey project. Our wonderful sweet funny smart dog Johnny had been dead only three months and here were my stupid brothers just hopping to pick out a new puppy.

Dad was even in on it; he's the one who took us out to that ranch to see the litter. Blue heelers are cow dogs, you know.

Harry was smiling so big he was practically sparkling as he watched that little fuzzy toot tumbling through the straw in the pony shed, kii-yii-ing and determined to make it all the way to where we were standing. The other little dogs were not even paying any attention, just rolling around over there by their mom. One of 'em was even asleep.

"*This* one," Harry hollered—he hollers all the time—and he couldn't wait any longer. He flopped into the straw himself and scooped the little ol' thing up.

"Here, Rose, here—he's the one!"

He thrust the puppy at me so fast that I couldn't do anything but take him. Softest stuff on earth, I bet, puppy fur. Luke peeled himself off the shed wall and started petting on him, too. Luke is a Teen-ager now and thinks he's hot stuff, so he always tries to be real casual.

While I was still standing there with my teeth set and my arms full of puppy, Dad and the boys headed for the car. Dad said something to the rancher and I scrambled after them, wagging that little dog. I had lost Round One for sure.

Dad was driving straight to Doc Grant's so we could make sure the little guy was healthy before we took him home as our own dog. Doc was a pal of Dad's as well as our veterinarian. He had tried hard to save our real dog, Johnny, but Johnny was pretty old in dog years. Mama and Dad had him before they even had us, except Luke, who was only a baby when they got Johnny. Harry and I didn't know any life without our dog.

"I guess we better just name this puppy John Wesley Hardin, too, because you know good and well we'll be calling him Johnny by mistake all the time anyway, both of 'em being blue heelers and all," Luke was saying.

"All *riiight!*" Harry hollered. Gaa, we're moving along in the closed-up car and there he is, hollering. He's such a wart. But then, he's only seven. "John Wesley Hardin Two, too!"

You may not remember who John Wesley Hardin was, but we live in Texas where everybody knows about him. He was a very famous Texas outlaw whose daddy was a Methodist preacher. But John went bad in spite of his name and he had killed forty-two men by the time he was thirty-five and once he shot a man for snoring. I love history. I'm probably going to be a history teacher when I grow up. Or a lawyer, like Dad.

The folks had named our Johnny that because blue heelers are so brave and strong and also kind of outlaw dogs. They are real sneaky and real good at conning their humans out of special treats and stuff.

My heart weighed about ninety pounds—which

is more than I do—at the very thought of calling this twerp by Johnny's own name, but I could see that it was two out of three, and even Dad was agreeing that we'd probably slip up and call the puppy the wrong name anyway. Maybe I could think of it as sort of a memorial to the real Johnny.

But you should have seen this new one on the examining table. It's shiny stainless steel, ice-cold to the touch, and when we set him up there for Doc to go over him, his little toenails slipped and he plopped on the cold table on his fat little tummy and started kii-yii-ing like crazy. Brave, my rear! No more like John Wesley Hardin the outlaw or Real Johnny Dog than the man in the moon. I could have puked. Everybody else thought it was real cute and they were all laughing.

Every time now that I get upset about something it makes me think about Mama and I want to cry. I don't want you to feel sorry for us, but it wasn't only Real Johnny who had died. There was something a whole lot worse, even. We had lost our mama in March. And then Johnny in June. So all summer there had just been Dad and Luke and Harry and me, moping around all the time. The boys had tried to be manly, but I mostly just gave over to it. My mama was perfect and I didn't know if I could stand it without her. Grandmother had come up and stayed with us for a while and she kept saying, "Rose-love, we're still a family, honey." But it didn't seem like it to me. Without Mama, and then with no Johnny either, that was just about all *any* of us could take.

"What're you going to name him, Rose?" Doc asked, putting his arm around my shoulders.

"John Wesley Hardin," I whispered. I was miserable.

"Ki-*yii!*" the puppy went, and Doc, who'd looked real quickly at me and started to say something, turned his attention back to the puppy and chuckled.

"John Wesley Hardin, the toughest gun in Texas," Doc laughed, sliding his warm hand under that cold little tummy. And of course the puppy quit crying right away and Doc never did say anything about that puppy getting Real Johnny's name when all he was was a babified coward.

That's the name Doc put on his vet papers, and where it says "Owner," Doc put *Rose* Marlin. Wow. I guess you can't put three names, maybe. The boys didn't act like they noticed anything unusual, but it weighed me down even more. Seemed like it kind of made me responsible for this ol' baby dog I didn't even want.

I sighed and picked him up. He was wiggling like a live fish except that he had these little baby needle claws, almost like a kitty, and he was scratching the phoo out of my arms. I sure did want to swat him—he drew blood in a couple of places, even—but I didn't think that would be a good idea so I squeezed him real hard instead. He sure was soft, and as soon as he got settled down from squeezing, he tipped right off to sleep in my arms.

When we got home, Dad helped us fix up a pen in the kitchen for him. We'd all have to take turns taking care of him and we knew that already. We have a chore chart at our house. It's a calendar where you take turns putting your name down for fixing supper or doing the dishes or vacuuming. We have to clean our own rooms, too, of course. We started the chore chart the first time Mama went to the hospital and then she never did really get well enough that we didn't need it.

We'd been taking care of the puppy that way for about a month when Luke said, "I'm going to get us a dog training book. He's real smart, but he sure needs work to know as much as First Johnny."

"All blue heelers are smart. *Real* Johnny was special," I said. It still hurt to talk about him, even. It seemed disloyal to me that we even got the same kind of dog. If the boys just had to have another dog, we should have got something different, not have it seem like any old blue heeler would do.

"Look how fast we got him housebroken! Johnny's a good boy," warbled Harry.

And it was barely out of his mouth that Johnny was good when we heard this huge crash in the boys' room. We raced in and there was Johnny, *in* Luke's wastebasket, mining for Kleenex. The crash we heard was him turning it over. *That's* a blue heeler for you, for sure. He *loves* Kleenex, especially—don't gag—used Kleenex, and there he was sitting in a pile of trash papers, munching away.

Harry snatched him up and spanked him good. Soon as he set him down, Johnny started going around in circles, looking at his tail. We cracked up. Even me.

"He thinks his tail did it! His *tail* got him in trouble." Luke was still laughing.

"Well, that's where I swatted him and I bet he doesn't eat Kleenex anymore," Harry said proudly.

Wrong. But he does try not to when Harry's around.

"Do you have homework tonight?" Dad asked, coming in while we were still picking up Johnny's torn-up snack. "I'm going over to the Kregers' for a while. They're having some people in to meet one of the new teachers. From Harry's school, in fact," he said.

"Miss Lakin? That's my teacher." Harry looked up.

"No. I think they said her name is Miss Welman.

Be in bed by ten now, Rose, Luke. Nine for you,
Harry. I may even be home by then."

I don't know why on earth we have to go to bed
so early. I'm nearly eleven years old, for Pete's sake.
And we had fixed Thanksgiving dinner all by ourselves this year, with me mostly in charge. Dad,
some. But mostly me.

And did you catch that about Dad meeting a new
teacher named Miss Welman? I sure didn't at the
time. But it had started, right then, that night in late
November. The main thing I want to tell you about.

Chapter 2

It was sometime in February when Dad directly mentioned Miss Welman to us again. The Grants were going to have a party at their house, just like they used to when Mama was here. Us kids were always included, too, and each family brought part of the meal. But there hadn't been one of those evenings in way more than a year. It would be my best friend, Katie, and her folks and her sister, and Mr. and Mrs. Sleidof and their twin two-year-olds; all the people the folks had run around with would be there.

The night before the party, Dad marshaled us all together in the kitchen to make the potato salad we were going to take. We'd already taken Johnny's pen down since he was housebroken now, so he was right underfoot, all fat and roly-poly. While we were boiling eggs and chopping onions and pickles and peeling potatoes, Dad said, "Tomorrow night, you're going to meet a nice woman that the Kregers introduced me to. She teaches at Harry's school."

Harry said, "Who?" realizing immediately that he was about to be the authority in the following matter.

Luke said nothing. I said nothing. But I wasn't quiet because I had caught on. I had *not* caught on. Luke had.

"Her name is Marie Welman. She teaches third-grade math and computer science. She moved here last summer from Indiana."

"So?" said ol' Luke, hacking away at the onions.

"So? What? What do you mean?"

"It's a regular old family covered dish like we used to do all the time, right? So who's this lady?"

Dad looked funny. He wiped his hands on a paper towel and put one hand on Luke's shoulder like suddenly this was going to be a Man-To-Man. After all, Luke *is* nearly fifteen. Harry put down his paring knife where he'd been going after the potato peels and he said, "Is she real redheaded? And about Mama's size?"

Dad flinched, but he carried on. "Yes. Red hair. I think she's thinner than Mama."

He didn't really gulp before he said "than Mama,"

but he did make some sort of odd little sound. Now I began to get it. It just hadn't ever even occurred to me before. I never even thought of such a thing. Can you imagine my being so dumb? I watch TV. I read. I live in the real world.

We have nine thousand friends whose parents are divorced. And their single parents date. And marry new people. I mean, seriously, I bet I have at least ten or eleven good friends who have double parents. That's what we call it here when you live with your mother and stepfather and go to your father and stepmother's for Christmas or part of the summer or something. We call it double parents. But our family couldn't be like that. We aren't divorced.

Harry said, "I see her in the hall. I don't have her."

Luke said, "Is she a fox?"

Dad looked worse than he had a minute ago. "What in the world does *that* mean?"

Now Luke started doing that funny thing he does with about a count of seven between words. He isn't dyslexic. Mama had him tested. And he makes real good grades. He's read everything in the entire school library, I bet. But sometimes when he is in a conversation, he'll talk with strange long gaps between words. He said, "Is she a"—one, two, three, four, five, six, seven—"desirable woman?"

I nearly cut myself with the paring knife on the pickles.

"*Fox*," Dad said, v-e-r-y carefully, "is a word which, in my time, meant smart, maybe even devious. Miss Welman is intelligent, but she is not devious. As to desirability, if that is what the word *fox* means in *your* time, I'm not sure I can testify. I desire to have her eat some of this potato salad and meet my children. Is that your question?"

His tone was not quite Courtroom, but it wasn't far off. Luke and Harry and I know this tone very well. It's the one he uses when we are just about in trouble but not quite. We can stay clean if we can make ourselves clear that we didn't mean what he thinks we mean and what we probably did mean until we realized that meaning it would get us in trouble.

Harry said, "Well, if you are going to invite somebody to eat with us, why don't you invite Miss Lakin? I *do* have her."

Harry hadn't caught on. But what can you expect at his age?

"Maybe another time I will," Dad said, smiling. "I haven't met Miss Lakin."

Harry extolled her virtues. (Maybe he'd not only caught on but was ahead of me and Luke.) "Miss Lakin is blonde," he said, "and she has a pet gerbil on her desk."

That night, after the potato salad was finished and stowed in the refrigerator, and Dad and Harry were doing Harry's homework, Luke and I held a Council in my room. That's what we call it in our family when you have to talk something over.

"Is this a date?" I demanded. "Do you think that's really what this is?"

"Sure. What did you think? You don't understand a thing about men," Luke said, acting like he already was one.

"I don't appreciate it being shoved down our throats. If he wants to take this computer expert to the movies, fine. But not to supper with all of us. Good grief, what are we supposed to say to her?"

"Maybe he's already taken her to the movies."

"*When?*"

"How should I know? I don't follow him around. He said the Kregers introduced him. He said she teaches school, she moved here from Indiana. He knows enough about her that he didn't just run into her yesterday on the street."

"And he kept her a secret from us!" I wailed.

"Rose, he's going to come in from a date and get us up and tell us everything he did and said and everything she did and said? *Not.*"

"But I don't want to meet her."

"But you wanted to know if he'd been to the movies with her before. You wanna be"—one, two, three, four, five, six, seven—"a part of whatever this is or not?"

"I don't even want to go to the Grants' now! I'd rather stay home by myself," I snapped.

As it turned out that's exactly what I did.

Chapter 3

I didn't even have to fake it. I woke up the next morning with an awful stomachache, before day-light. I had to get out of bed and throw up. Seemed like I barely had another nap when I had to get up and do it again. Dad heard me and got the Pepto Bismol. He remembered about the dry toast and the Coke, all the things Mama used to do if any of us threw up.

I slept off and on all day, but even though I didn't throw up anymore after about noon, Dad decreed I better not go to the party. He put the Grants' phone number by my bed and everybody but Johnny Dog and I left. I drifted off to sleep again.

Next thing I knew was when I felt Luke sit down on my bed.

"Rose? You awake? You gonna puke or can you talk?"

I maintained I wasn't going to puke and I could talk. I sat up against the pillows. Luke's feet were hanging off the bed and New Johnny was chewing on his shoelaces.

"Well, she's not bad."

I came wide awake. The dinner! Miss Welman!

"Doc was on one of his real funny kicks and the food was real good. Mrs. Kreger got mad at the Sleidof twins because they got into her purse. They got her lipstick and eye shadow and were trailing Tums all over the house. . . ."

Luke talks so slow, and he *will not* get to the point on stories.

". . . Miss Welman helped chase them and get Mrs. Kreger's stuff put back together, but what really got away with Mrs. Kreger was that the twins' mother didn't even spank them or anything. She just kept laughing about it."

"What does she *look* like?"

"Everybody was laughing, even Mrs. Grant, and there was lipstick on the rug in the family room and everything—"

"LUKE! Is she pretty?"

Luke grinned and had the awesome nerve to say, "You know Mrs. Grant. What do you mean, is she pretty?"

If I hadn't been sick as a dog, I'd have thrown the pillow at him or jumped out of bed and hit him. He could tell I was about to blow up. He got up and went over and sat in the chair by my desk, out of reach, and started fiddling with my cartoon calendar and the pencils on the desk and all.

"She's okay. She's real clean," he said slowly.

"WHAT DOES SHE *LOOK* LIKE?" Rats, I thought, if he starts doing that count-of-seven thing, I'm outa this bed clobbering him, no matter whether I'm sick or not.

"Just like Harry said. Redheaded. Tall. Skinny."

"How old is she? She's not a bimbo, is she?" Boy, I hadn't thought of that possibility, either, till that very second—that Dad might get taken in by a bimbo.

"I don't know. Thirty, at least. Probably not quite as old as Mama. Was."

"Is it *Miss*, really? Or *Ms.?* Did she say anything about being married before?"

Now Harry would have answered that question directly. But no, no, not ol' Luke. *He* said, "I don't think she has any children. The way she carried on with the twins—"

That set me off again. "Oh great. Good. Fine. I hadn't even thought about that yet. I was just thinking about if she was that old and never had been married, she's probably a dog . . ." *Instead of a fox*, I'd started to say, and that got me tickled in spite of everything and I started halfway giggling, but ol' Luke was plodding onward, ever onward.

". . . She got some hand lotion and Kleenex out of her purse and wiped the lipstick off of 'em and everything. She talked quite a bit, but she never did mention an ex-husband." He'd finally caught up to the question. "Usually, when she'd be talking to somebody else, Dad'd be looking at her. Like he was listening to her, wherever else in the room he was, or like he was trying to figure her out."

I groaned.

"She'd tell about what-all she did in Indiana before she came here. Not bragging, or acting like where she lived before was better, but just telling about it. She didn't mention any men, though."

Luke looked off into space a minute. I waited to see if he was through. He wasn't.

"Dad'd be talking racketball to Doc and Mr. Kreger, and she was over on the couch with Mrs. Kreger and Mrs. Sleidof, and they'd be talking about work. Mrs. Sleidof said they're going to remodel the offices where she is at the bank. But Dad would be cutting his eyes over at Miss Welman and she'd know he was watching her. This is hard to describe.

She wasn't talking for his benefit, but I know she knew he was looking at her."

"RatsRatsRats."

"She wasn't a put-on. I didn't mean that."

"I should have been there."

"What for? I'm telling you all about it."

"But look, this single woman from out of state comes down here and right away she's running around with this . . . this . . . Eligible Man! She probably never had a date in her life before! Of *course* she's putting on for him. Luke, I'm practically a woman already my own self, and I know that's so. Oh, Luke, good grief, our *dad* is a PRIZE CATCH!"

"So this is it, then, huh, the new thing?"

"*What? The what?*"

"He's"—count of seven—"dating. Dad's dating, for sure. I knew it was bound to start sometime."

"*I* never thought it was bound to. Why does he have to?"

"Well. He has to. This woman might not be . . . important. But there will be one someday who is." He put the calendar down and lumbered to the door.

"G'night," he said.

"Take New Johnny with you!" I hissed. And he picked the old fluffball up on his way out.

I flopped over on my stomach and slid down under the pillows and covers. Luke had called her "this woman." He didn't really say it as if he thought of her as The Enemy, but to me she was. Poor Dad. The perfect victim. I would have to think of something.

Chapter 4

I felt fine the next day. Katie came over that afternoon and we got to wrestling around with Johnny Dog. Katie's real stylish and she had a bandanna around her hair. We took it off and put it on Johnny. You wouldn't believe it, but he *loved* it! Have you ever heard of a vain dog? He must have thought he looked real cute or something. When we took it off him, he started bump-bumping Katie's hand with his nose, like he wanted it back. We cracked up, and she put it back on him. You know, around his neck like a cowboy. Like John Wesley Hardin, probably.

He ran around in circles and rolled over and everything, but he didn't try to rub it off. Luke told him to sit, like we'd learned how to do in the dog training book, and he did it, but then he leaped right back up and started running and playing some more.

"I think we better send Johnny to school," Luke said.

Harry died laughing.

"There's an ad in the paper. Dog obedience school. I think he ought to go."

"How much does it cost? We have the book."

"It's a class. Five dollars a class, I think it was, but you have to agree to go every time. I bet Dad would like for us to do it."

"He *is* pretty silly. I mean, he sat, but it was like he'd done what we asked him to, so that was enough and he got right back up and started doing what *he* wanted to do again. He didn't seem like he knew he was supposed to stay sitting until we gave him permission to get up," I said.

"Miss Welman likes dogs," Harry said suddenly. My stomach squeezed up for the first time all day.

"Your dad was sure cute with her last night," Katie said. "He just kept grinning and watching her—"

"What on earth for? He doesn't know her from a rabbit," I snapped, with my stomach rippling up and down like a kite in a downdraft.

"It sure *looked* like he knows her pretty well," said Katie, looking confused. "Has she been over to spend the night yet?"

There's a girl in our class whose mom's boyfriend spends the night a lot. The mom thinks her daughter and all of us don't know it, but of course we do.

"No," Luke and I said at practically the same time.

"No," I said again and wanted to say, "And she ain't gonna," but I didn't want to give Katie the satisfaction of knowing I didn't approve in case she'd only mentioned it to get my goat. That's the thing about Katie. She tries to sound like she's teasing, but sometimes she's really after your hide. Instead, I said, "I'll ask Dad if we should take Johnny to obedience school. After all, he's *my* dog, on his vet papers."

Okay, okay. I know that wasn't very nice, but how can you be a nice person if you're worried all the time?

Chapter 5

"Do you all want to take Johnny out to the lake?" Dad asked us the next Saturday. It had been a pretty normal week—no more Welman nonsense.

We all got in the car, with an old towel on the seat for Johnny, and roared out there. He loves to chase the ball at the lake. He must be part otter because he sure does like the water. He loves the sprinkler in the yard and he loves to go to the lake.

It was a pretty chilly day, but Luke threw the ball in the water anyway and Johnny hightailed it right in after it and swam like he thought he could make Paris by dark. We didn't stay too long, and we dried him off good so he wouldn't catch cold.

All the way home, I thought Dad would say that he had another date that night. I even had the mean thought that maybe he took us all out to the lake so he could get us in a good mood before he informed us he had a date. It *was* Saturday. Grudgingly, I had to admit to myself that I was probably the only one who'd need to be in a good mood to hear that news. The boys didn't seem to care nearly as much as I did. It sure is hard to tell your own self the truth sometimes.

But he didn't say a word and he was home watching movies with us that night. It was two weeks before he took Miss Welman out again, as far as I know. After school on that Friday, he called home and said, "Rose, can you and the boys handle supper without me? I'm thinking of taking Miss Welman out to dinner."

"Sure. Have you already called her?"

"Yes. Why?"

"Well. I thought maybe you'd like to . . . Did you ever do anything about Miss Lakin?"

"Who?"

"You know. That other teacher Harry was talking about. Maybe you—maybe you oughta meet a variety, maybe." My heart was thudding. I felt ridiculous. But I wanted to get it said. I'd decided there might be safety in numbers, like the great battle generals say. After all, he's known this Welman woman for about five months, best I can tell, and also as far as I know, he hasn't taken any other women out.

There was a little pause before Dad answered me.

"Well. I'm not conducting a survey. I'm sure Miss Lakin is very nice, but I don't know her. Why don't I invite Miss Welman to dinner at our house some night? I think you'd enjoy her company, too."

"Okay," I said. What else *could* I say?

At supper that night, I tried to hold a Council with the boys.

"Dad is out with Miss Welman again. This makes three times that we know of for sure," I began ominously.

"So?" Luke didn't even stop eating or look at me. It had been his turn to cook, so he had made mac and cheese. He loves any kind of pasta.

"Well, I just think we need to look into it. I, for one, am against it."

Harry started laughing. He also gave Johnny a bite under the table, which we don't allow and which he thought I didn't see.

"Dad's got a girlfriend! Dad's got a girlfriend!" he started singing. And I burst into tears. Johnny got between my feet as I was running to my room and I nearly fell down, to make it even more undignified. I slammed the door and really set up a howl. I couldn't help it. I was bawling like crazy. What was the deal here? Am I the only one who remembers we *had* a mother? I was crying into ol' Johnny's neck and he was twisting around, taking bites of my hair, which pulled, so I cried more. You know how, if you're already feeling bad, a little pain really gets away with you? I quit hugging him and shoved him away.

Real Johnny would never have done that. He always realized when you felt bad and did not do any funny stuff to you. I felt *so* bad, I wished we didn't have New Johnny, even though I'd got to where I liked him okay. He wasn't half the dog that Real Johnny was, and I resented his being with us. I was getting rolling on what probably would have been an all-night cry when Luke opened the door without knocking and came in. He sat me straight up on the bed, held onto my shoulders, and looked right into me.

"Rose, stop it. Right now." His voice sounded odd, like maybe in another minute he'd cry, too, but he didn't.

"Mama's never coming back. You've got to face it. If Dad doesn't take Miss Welman out, he'll take somebody else out. He's gonna have adult company. We better just hope it's always somebody as nice as she is."

He stopped, and his breathing was so shuddery

that even New Johnny settled down. Without saying another syllable, Luke led me into the bathroom, got a washrag real wet, wrung it out, and
swung it around by one corner to get it cool, like
Mama used to when we had a fever. Then he put it
very gently on my face. After my eyes were covered
up and I couldn't see him, he actually kissed me on
the forehead, and then he said, "Get in there and
help Harry clean up. It's your turn."

Chapter 6

The next week was when dog obedience school started for Johnny. It was puppy pre-k, actually, because he was only six months old, but he was so rambunctious that Dad had agreed we'd better go ahead and enroll him so we could get him under control.

He was getting so big. Of course, he eats everything that doesn't eat him first. And he's tall. Almost as tall then as Real Johnny ever got in his whole life. But Real Johnny had been the runt of his litter.

At dog school, you have to name a designated handler. What I mean is, it couldn't be the three of us taking turns each week teaching him. They wanted you to name one person as handler and that same person had to take him in the ring at every class. I thought it might as well be Dad, since he would have to drive one of us down there to class every time anyway—they hold the school on the parking lot of one of the banks downtown near Dad's office—but Dad designated Luke and ruled that we should all go and watch (which they let you do if you don't talk or move around much) so that we would all learn the lessons.

Good thing. They even gave Johnny homework. He had to have certain supplies like a choke collar and a leather lead, six feet long. Also, they gave us a batch of Xeroxed handouts the first night about what he'd be learning. He'd learn to heel, sit, and stay, primarily. I figured if he learned "Stay" and "Don't Jump Up" and that was all, it would be well worth it. But they didn't have a command named Don't Jump Up.

We'd be going to dog school every Wednesday night, and we didn't want Johnny to look bad, so we started right in on the homework when we got home from class that night.

There we were, walking him down the street on his new lead, when this lady in a big blue car screeched to a halt and yelled out, "Hey, you kids! How did you get that raccoon on that leash?"

Can you stand it? And I hate it when some dopey

grown-up says stuff like "you kids." I yelled right back, "He's a DOG! A baby blue-heeler DOG!" Made me furious. Even though he does have rings on his silly ol' fluffy tail. I don't know why the boys looked at each other with Luke grinning and rolling his eyes at Harry, either, when I grabbed him up and defended him. Who did that woman think she was? She wasn't all that gorgeous her own self.

Chapter 7

The very first Saturday after we started dog school, Dad brought Miss Welman home to dinner. He said he would do steaks on the outdoor grill and we would make the rest of the food.

It would be the meal that we had perfected as a team for the first night of Grandmother's visits: little filets, bacon-wrapped, that Dad does on the grill, fresh mushrooms sauteed so they make a sauce for the steak, baked potatoes with sour cream (yogurt, really) and chives for people to put in them, and a big tossed salad with two or three store-bought dressings to choose from (only we put them in little bowls with dipper spoons on the table).

Mama never would let us put any bottles of anything, including ketchup, on the table, even when we ate in the kitchen. She said it looked gross and it was part of our learning table manners not to eat with the loaf of bread or the bottle of mustard sitting there in front of us like a truck-stop café.

How Dad introduced the topic of having Miss Welman over to dinner was by asking if any of us had made plans for Saturday night. He said if we had, we could keep the plans; he would take us wherever we were supposed to go if we had a practice for something at school or we'd already cemented something with friends. He said it was no big deal. He said he was just having a friend over.

He said that, and words to that effect, several times. It was pretty funny to realize that Dad was that nervous.

Well, we none of us had other plans.

But I was trying to make one.

At first I thought I'd do something awful to the food. I'd put vinegar in the mushrooms or something so that they'd taste bad and ruin the steak and she would think that we were real dumb or careless and she wouldn't want to have anything to do with Dad anymore. But family pride prevailed. This was one of our best meals, and I couldn't bring myself to foul it up.

Then I thought about maybe being rude. Not exactly full-blown rude enough to bring Dad down

on my case, but just not accommodating. Saying
"um" a lot and "you know"—as in "I'm—um—in
the—um—kitchen, y'know, and —um . . ." Lots of
people do that, adults even, and actually think
they're making sense. She wouldn't in a million
years catch on that I was just doing it to be annoy-
ing. Dad would, though.

First thing Saturday morning, he tore out of the
driveway like his shirt was on fire, to go get groceries for this Date Dinner. Luke and I did Johnny's
homework with him, one at a time, so that he did it
twice, and Harry started work on teaching him to
roll over for a cookie the way Real—I mean *First*—
Johnny could.

Harry is a wizard with animals. He lay down on
the kitchen floor with the cookie—it's a Milk-Bone,
really, not a cookie for people—and tapped it on the
floor. Johnny lay down practically nose to nose with
him, wiggling and trying to bite the cookie. Harry
said, "Roll over." And *he* rolled over, himself. Real
slow, so that Johnny's nose, following the cookie,
made him roll over, too.

I realize you are going to find this hard to believe,
but I already told you that blue heelers are smart: it
only took Harry twenty-two minutes to teach that
puppy to roll over. I swear. And by then Harry was
standing up, holding the cookie, and saying "Roll

over" in a calm normal voice, and that baby dog was rolling like a log going downhill.

We used up nearly a box of Milk-Bones by the time we'd all tried it two or three times with him, and he was practically waddling, but it sure was fun.

By the time we'd played with Johnny most of the day, it seemed like, and also done our regular Saturday stuff like clean up our rooms, it was time to get ready for the Big Din-Din. Dad had already sort of sauntered out to the grill to get it going.

Chapter 8

I beat the boys to the bathroom and did the whole number: long, hot soaky bubble bath, washed my hair and blew it dry.

First I decided to wear a blue and white striped skirt and a blue T-shirt. Then I decided that was too dressed up. I wanted to look like it was just another Saturday night as far as I was concerned. I took off the skirt and T-shirt and put on some jeans and a green sweatshirt. Then I decided that was going to be too hot. I put the skirt and T-shirt back on. I have some of those fat little silver hearts on a chain that everybody on earth has, so I put those on, too.

She had on a long-sleeved cotton dress, paisley, with a lace collar and some gold shrimp earrings. Real cute shoes. She is sure enough a redhead and okay-looking but not gorgeous. She is thin as a stick and her hair looks like it's either naturally curly or she has a very good curly perm.

Johnny jumped all over her the minute Dad opened the door, but Luke was on him like a shot, yelling, "Sit! Sit!" and grabbing at him.

She reacted quickly. Johnny jumped up, she kneed him. Kneed *at* him. That's what you're supposed to do. Except that Johnny is so fast he can run a hole in the wind, so you nearly always miss. She missed. But I'll hand it to her. She knew what you were supposed to do, and she didn't have a fit because her dress got jumped on.

Dad put her on the screened porch, so he could keep tabs on her and the grill both. Harry hung on her. I said I had to be in the kitchen.

I did have to be. Some. I could see her and Harry and Dad out the big window, of course. Luke was trying to keep Johnny under control, so he was sort of moving around wherever Johnny popped up.

Seemed like Miss Welman liked Johnny. This was the first time she'd met him, and of course Harry had to show her the cookie trick right away. I told him he shouldn't give Johnny any more cookies, as many as he'd had that afternoon, but he did it anyway. And of course she thought it was darling. It *is* darling. Who wouldn't think so?

Then Luke had to show her that Johnny could go get the ball and "fetch" and pretty soon when I looked out the window, there they all were, throwing the ball for Johnny, the world's happiest dog, center of his universe, catching the ball in midair, jumping all over everybody, all of them laughing, with steak smells everywhere and the sun shining and the little peach tree in bloom. I even heard her telling Johnny how cute his bandanna was. We had got him his own red one and he pranced around in it every day.

I wanted to cry.

I wanted to spoil it. I wanted to go outside and swat Johnny, this stinky little puppy who couldn't even play Frisbee like First Johnny was an absolute champion of. I wanted to slam every dish in Mama's kitchen up against the wall.

"Okay, time to go inside and get your plates, the meat's ready," Dad called merrily. "And leave Johnny out here—I don't want any begging at the table."

"I want to sit by Rose," *she* said. "I haven't even helped her or visited with her—you guys have let me be rude!" And she came running in, washing her hands in the kitchen sink, helping me put stuff on the dining room table. Dad brought her plate and her steak in, of course. And there we sat, next to each other, visiting about school and everything.

You're thinking that I just gave up. She sat by me and talked to me like a person, so you're thinking I just lapped it up and fell right into her plan to kidnap our dad. No. I didn't do that.

In fact, there was only one time that whole evening when I could halfway stand her.

There we were, after dinner, loading the dishwasher and trying to be chipper with each other and she said, "I have this student named Long Day. Isn't that a wonderful name?"

I said it sure was, and how in the world . . . ? (Rinse, rinse, rinse.)

"He was his mom's first baby. He started being born very early one morning and his dad rushed his mom to the hospital, where she labored all day long, getting more and more tired and discombobulated, with him trying to be born. When he finally was, they asked her what name she'd picked out for him, and all she could say, over and over, was 'Long day, long day,' so that's what they thought she wanted to put on his birth certificate. She had intended to name him Elbert if he was a boy, so now his full name is Long Day Elbert Jennings. Everybody calls him Long Day. He says he likes it better than Elbert."

"Well, who wouldn't?" I said. "Elbert is awful."

But she had me. I couldn't resist. "Does Long Day just tell that story all the time, if anybody asks him about his name?" (Stack, stack, stack.)

"Yes. I think he likes it. It doesn't seem to embarrass him at all. And now he has two brothers and a sister, all of whom have plain names."

"What are they?" We had all the dishes in the machine now and she was scrubbing the grill thing from outdoors, even though Dad kept butting in and telling her she didn't have to do that.

"His sister's name is Louisa Nella, but I don't know his brothers."

"I don't think Louisa Nella is exactly plain."

"Well. No. But it certainly isn't Nosmo King."

That got me, big time. I laughed like crazy. You've probably heard that story about the woman who named her baby Nosmo King because the last thing she saw on her way into the hospital was a sign that said No Smoking, and she thought it said Nosmo King. It's supposed to have happened right here, but Dad says it didn't. He says it is an urban legend, which is what you call a made-up story that has been told all around the country as a supposedly real happening.

But, see, here's the thing: Miss Welman could tell good stories and I love that. *And*, she knew exactly how old I am, but she told me that story about the lady having her baby just like I was a grown woman.

Then she brought up the Nosmo King story, like she already knew I was well enough informed that I'd heard it, too. I had to give her some points.

She acted like a semidecent person. But I did *not* entirely fall for it.

There is this kid in my grade who is very excellent with math, and one day in English class, when he was asked to define *capitulate*, he said to the teacher, "I can't. I'm not a word person. I'm a numbers man."

The teacher looked real funny, and then she said, "No, I guess you're not a word person, or you'd know that a numbers man is *not* the same thing as a boy who is good at mathematics."

She did not say what a numbers man is, but I asked Dad that night and he said it's a gambler. I wouldn't know much about that. I don't think they let people gamble in Texas. Except the lottery.

But I *am* a word person. In fact, I'm the one that day who held up my hand to define *capitulate*, and what I'm telling you right now is that I did not capitulate. I was polite to Miss Welman, but I didn't buy her program one hundred percent.

When I went to bed that night, my head was spinning with the sound of her calling Dad "Ben." It's his name of course, but it seemed so . . . *intimate*.

I imagined them having a conversation about marrying each other. Maybe she'd say, *"Ben*, I don't want to marry you. I like Luke and Harry but I can't stand Rose."

I imagined him begging her to anyway and maybe saying that I was not so bad—or maybe saying that he'd see if he could get Grandmother to take me off their hands! Then I imagined her saying she loved us all, and our house was great, and our dog was great, and when were they going to get married? And *him* saying, *"Married?* But I just had you over to dinner—what do you mean, Get Married?"

I was tossing and turning and really letting my mind run wild. Johnny crawled up on the foot of the bed. I knew it, but I didn't pay any attention to him. He stretched out full-length beside me, on the outside of the covers, and pushed against me. Suddenly, I realized that he might, might, might make as good a dog as First Johnny. Here I was in a turmoil, and there he was, quietly, firmly, definitely, *with* me.

Chapter 9

I think it was at the very next lesson that he did such a great thing at dog school.

All the dogs were supposed to be learning sit-stay. We had been doing his homework with him every evening, faithfully. Actually he probably got more homework done than anybody else because first Luke would do it with him, and then me, and then Harry. Sometimes Dad would even do it once with him. The teacher had told us that we could bribe him to do his lessons with tidbits—well, she didn't say "bribe," she said "reward"—but we had voted against doing that. We give him his Milk-Bone when he rolls over, which is a trick, but we decided that we wanted him to sit-stay and down-stay and heel and come just because he was told to, and not be able to get mad and blow up and not do it if we didn't happen to have a treat handy at the time.

We got to school that night and lined up on the curb with the other guests. Nearly every dog had a friend or two besides the designated handler. Luke was our handler, you know, and he took ol' Johnny into the ring.

He was between two rottweiler puppies, a brother and sister who belonged to the same couple; the man had one of them and the woman had the other one. In front of the first rottweiler was a real skinny, sleek pure black Doberman, and behind the second rottweiler was a fat little German shepherd, maybe even younger than Johnny but bigger. So in that company, Johnny was the smallest dog.

There were some little ones on the other side of the ring, but nearest to him, they were all bigger and it had the effect on him of cowing him a little bit. He acted pretty nice, not nearly so bouncy and Chairman of the World as he does at home.

They all plodded around in a big circle for a while, heeling and sitting, heeling and sitting. Except that "heel" for most of them was a joke. They'd roar out to the end of their leads and their handlers would jerk 'em back. Then they'd want to visit with the dog behind them and their handlers would jerk them forward. Most of them would sit pretty well, but they couldn't make themselves stay very long.

For the very last thing in class, the teacher said all the dogs were going to play a game called Monkey in the Middle. The big circle of dogs would keep on going around, but in turn each dog would go into the center of the circle and that dog's handler would make him sit. Then the handler would go out to the end of the lead (you weren't allowed to ever, ever let go of the lead at dog school) and the puppy would have to sit-stay while the circle of other puppies walked around him until his handler said, "Okay," and then he could get up and be petted and loved on.

My heart sank. There was no way ol' Johnny would do that and we were all going to be embarrassed and Luke would have to be stern, which Luke hates and which he is not very good at. Harry, now, Harry can be stern. Come to think of it, maybe that's why he's such a good animal trainer.

The little bitty dogs across the circle from Johnny were first, and they were pretty awful. I began to feel better. It wouldn't be so sad for Johnny to be awful if he wasn't the only one. Then it was the Doberman's turn and she went uts-nay. She spun around and around and jumped up on her owner and boofed and hollered. She couldn't stand it, six feet away from him, in the middle of all those dogs walking around her. And, see, they were all puppies, too, and only in their third night at school, so their walking around in the big outside circle wasn't very dignified either. Some of them were also jumping around and boofing.

Next, the first rottweiler went out in the center. He sat down perfectly. His owner went out to the end of the lead, and here came the rotty after him. His owner took him back into center. He sat. His owner backed off to the end of the lead, and here came the rotty, to him again. They tried it about six times and finally slunk back to their place in the circle. The rotty wouldn't stay out there by himself, period.

Then it was our turn. Ol' Johnny and Luke left the circle and went into the center. Harry couldn't look. He had a piece of grass and was following an ant along the curb with it, trying to act like he didn't even know whose dog was in the middle. My heart was pounding and I imagine I had my nose pinched. Katie says when I am upset, I pinch my nose in, not with my hands or anything gross, but with the muscles in it, as if it actually grew thinner. Johnny sat. Luke bent down to him, petted him just a second, and went to the end of the lead.

I could hardly stand it. You'd think it was the Bi-district Play-offs. Harry sneaked a nonchalant peek. Johnny was sitting. Luke was standing at the far end of the lead. I looked at Harry, who cut his eyes at me and sort of widened them, which I guess meant, "Shut up. Don't breathe, even." We both looked back at the dogs.

The second rottweiler had bounced on by, and the fat little shepherd waddled by, being halfway dragged along because he was tired now and wanted to go home and have his supper, probably. Then the little bitty dogs were coming by, and a Pomeranian was dancing along on her hind legs part of the way. I called her the Majorette. I bet her cookie trick was to get up on her hind legs and that was about all she could do or wanted to do. No matter what the command at school was, the Majorette would just walk on her hind legs.

Still Johnny sat. He looked like a statue. His ears were up like satellite dishes, his tail was bushed out on the paving straight behind him, and he never took his big bright brown eyes off Luke's face. He was so still, his bandanna didn't even wiggle.

Listen, they circled him *twice*. I'm telling you the truth. They circled him *twice*, and finally the teacher said, "Release your dog," and Luke said, "Okay, Johnny, heel," and turned into the circle without looking back, like he just naturally knew that his dog would be right there, nose at his master's knee, heeling like a champ.

Boy, you should have seen Luke's face! I saw

right there what that phrase "the flush of victory" means. I was hoping I wasn't going to cry, I was so proud of both of them. Harry, of course, started looking for the ant, like the whole thing was nothing to him.

Dad had walked over to the office from where we'd parked at the dog school lot, and when he came back to the car, we fell all over ourselves trying to tell him how great Johnny had been. That is, Harry and I did. Luke just sat there, still pink in the face, grinning. Johnny had slung himself across the back floor, panting, and looking like he was grinning, too.

"Looks like you're going to make a pretty good trainer, Luke," Dad said.

"Well," said ol' Luke. "All I did was, when I petted him there after he first sat, I whispered in his ear, 'Johnny, you stay till I say heel, or I'm gonna beat the living stuffing out of you when I get you home.' "

Chapter 10

I suppose you know that dogs and cats have these little secret wristwatches. I don't know where they actually wear them, but it sure does seem like they have them. First Johnny knew exactly when bedtime came and he was supposed to get a cookie. Every night, even if he was sound asleep somewhere, he'd leap up wide awake and start pacing back and forth between wherever we were and the cabinet where his cookie box lives till somebody got him one. And now this Johnny is doing the same thing.

When we got home from dog school, he flopped down in the middle of everybody and went right to sleep. But sure enough, in about an hour, he leaped up and charged around boofing and bump-bumping us and flopping back down making that silly huffing sound he makes till finally I got him a cookie. He rolled over for it, of course.

"We oughta get him a present," Harry said. "He was so smart at his school and he learned to roll over and he can already tell time."

"He can't tell time, Harry; you know he can't. It's instinct, that's all." Luke didn't even look up from his book.

"But we could get him a present, couldn't we?"

"Sure. I guess. Why not?" Luke mumbled.

When Harry gets set on something, he doesn't shut up about it till either we do it or Dad says it's "out of the question," which is one of Dad's favorite ways to say no. But getting Johnny a present was fine with Dad, so in a day or two we all got in the car and whipped out to Wal-Mart to look for dog goodies. There we were in the aisle where they keep chew bones and fake candy for animals when Harry started yelling, "There's Miss Welman!"

And Dad spun around like he was on a too-tight spring.

"Marie! Hi!" he called, and here she came.

"We're gettin' Johnny a good-boy present!" Ol' Harry was hopping up and down.

"What kind of things does he like?" she asked.

My cow, I wanted to say, what do you think he

likes? He's a dog. He likes to eat and chew stuff. But Luke took it as a serious question.

"He likes treats and tennis balls, and he loves water."

"Water . . . well . . . now, there's a thought. . . ." She was looking up the aisle she'd come down.

Harry got it at once. Maybe he'd already seen them, too.

"A 'wimming pool!" he hollered. "We could get him a 'wimming pool!"

"SSSwimming pool," Dad and that woman said at the very same time. See, Harry used to couldn't say his S's, especially if there was a *w* after them, like *swimming* or *swoosh*, and sometimes still if he's real excited he doesn't say them right. But I couldn't believe she thought it was any of *her* business and furthermore she and Dad stood there and died laughing at how cute they were, saying "SSSwimming" at the same time. It gagged me with a spoon.

I put my arm around poor ol' Harry to lead him to the wading pool display, but he was too fired up to walk and didn't act like getting corrected by practically a total stranger bothered him at all. He ran on, nearly knocking over the rack of chew bones. Instead, *she* came up beside me and walked with me around the corner, still chuckling and sort of shaking her head.

"I'm so used to correcting kids in class," she said. "You don't suppose I hurt Harry's feelings?"

"No." I hated having to admit it, but it was the truth. He didn't act like he cared.

There were a million wading pools, all the way from smaller than a bathtub to so big that you probably could really swim in them. Harry wanted a green one and he and Dad were moving the stacks around to get to one that was about five feet across, real shallow, and green with frogs on it.

"Nine ninety-five!" Luke groused. "He better like it."

Harry tried to roll it up the aisle, but he was too short, so Luke carried it to the checkout counter. Dad was getting out the money and he said, "Marie, you want to come by the house and see if Johnny likes his present?"

"Well . . ." She looked over at me. I wasn't saying a word. I wasn't doing a darn thing. I was just standing there.

"No," she said. "I better not. I have some papers to grade."

So Dad paid for the pool and walked her out to her car while we wrestled the present into our car. You can bend those plastic pools but you have to be real careful so they don't crack.

Johnny was a nut about it. He didn't jump right

into it or anything, but what he did was play ball for a while and *then* jump in it, like to cool off. Luke and I threw the ball for him a bunch of times and then Harry was splashing his hands in the pool and that showed Johnny what to do, I guess. He plowed into it, nose first, bandanna immediately soaking wet, and shook himself kind of like birds do in a bird-bath. He was real funny.

"I wish Miss Welman had come," Harry squealed. "She'da liked ol' John in his ssswimming pool."

Suddenly I felt bad. Well. I know it wasn't *exactly* my fault. She had papers to grade. She said she did. But it is possible that maybe I didn't look too welcoming. I didn't like her jumping on Harry, though. Who did she think she was? I know she more or less apologized and I know it's a teacher's job to teach stuff. But still.

Chapter 11

Right after that, I got in the worst trouble I've ever been in in my life.

Dad hadn't seen much of Miss Welman since he had her over to dinner, as far as I knew. That was making me feel magnanimous toward her. I was thinking she wasn't so bad. He could have picked out one who was worse. So I didn't even get a big anxiety wave or anything when he took her to the movies every once in a while.

However, I was, as they say, lulled to sleep. Little did I know that the plot between them was thickening.

He came in from work one day and announced that he'd asked Mrs. Donnell to spend the night with us Saturday because he would be in Austin and

he wouldn't feel easy about us if we were by ourselves. Mrs. Donnell used to baby-sit when we were
little and while we certainly don't need a baby-sitter
anymore, I guess it's okay for when Dad's out of
town because none of us can drive yet, so we'd be in
a pickle if something went wrong. So we planned
that we'd rent a bunch of movies and we'd each have
one friend over to watch them with us. Katie could
come, and Harry asked Melvin Dietze, and then at
the last minute, Luke, as usual, said he'd forgotten
to ask anybody.

Dad took us to Albertson's Saturday morning and
we rented *Batman Returns* and *E.T.* and I got Lau-
rence Olivier in *Rebecca*. I say "I" got it because I had
to spring for it with my own money. Harry and
Luke wouldn't vote to use any of the money Dad
gave us to rent it, because they think it is icky which
it is not. It may be old and it is a love story, but it
is most certainly not icky. I supposed that they'd
probably want to watch it anyway, and then I'd
have this big ethical decision about whether or not
to let them, since they didn't help pay.

Mrs. Donnell's car was already in the driveway
when Dad drove us home, so he said, "I won't come
back in with you. Have a good time, and I'll see you
tomorrow when Miss Welman and I get home."

Lurch.

Whack.

Anxiety wave, big-time.

Can you feature him doing that? He was taking that woman to Austin with him for the weekend and did not bother to mention it to his own children till he was practically on I-35!

Rage is absolutely the only way to describe how I felt. I think I even know now what "seeing red" means. I was so mad I could hardly see anything. Luke and Harry and I all three just stood stock-still as he pulled out of the driveway and headed off down the street. Luke had the sack with the movies in it and he moved first.

"I guess he's sleeping with her," he mumbled as he started up the front steps.

"This guy in our school, his father—" Harry began, following him.

"Shut UP!" I hollered, and I ran past both of them, barreling into the living room, making this long low funny *zzzzzzzz* sound with my teeth gritted, forgetting all about how Mrs. Donnell was already in there. She was watching TV so I flew right on through to the screen porch, kicking Johnny off me and slamming the door. I stood there a minute, breathing hard, and going *zzzzz*, with Johnny still trying to jump all over me.

I could hear Luke saying, "She's okay, Mrs. Donnell. She's just mad that we made her pay her own money for this rotten movie she rented," and the boys followed me out onto the porch. Luke closed the door carefully and said at once, "He might *not* be sleeping with her."

"I don't care if he is! It's not that. It *is* that." I stomped out the screen door and into the yard, Johnny and the boys right after me.

"What do you care? This guy at my school, his—" Harry was bouncing along beside me as I marched up and down in the middle of the yard.

Mr. Burns was mowing his grass next door, so Luke hollered over the mower, "You don't know anything! All men and women sleep together. . . ," and of course at that very moment Mr. Burns turned off the mower to empty the basket and Luke was yelling across the neighborhood on a bright Saturday morning, "All Men and Women Sleep Together!"

Mr. Burns glanced over at us and turned the mower back on. There was absolutely no place we could go. Him out here. Mrs. Donnell in the house. Harry with us. You can't talk about stuff like that with a little boy around. I couldn't think straight anyway. Luke looked over at Mr. Burns, and took my elbow, and grabbed Harry by the shoulder, and steered us back to the porch. We huddled together on the settee at the far end away from the window and where we could hear each other softly over the mower.

I had stopped making *zzzzzzzz* noises and could see pretty well, so although I was still mad as a horned toad, I was able to realize that Luke was upset, too, and Harry's bottom lip was trembling.

"Did they go to a meeting down there?" Harry sort of whimpered. I expect it was mostly my fault that he was about to cry. I don't think he had any idea what the real deal was; I just think he knew good and well something awful was going on because of how *I* was acting. But I couldn't help it.

"Maybe they did," Luke said cautiously. "We don't know. Maybe that's why we're mad. He didn't tell us."

"I don't care if he *had* told us. It stinks and I will never speak to either of them again," I said.

Harry's eyes got big as he took in the enormity of that statement.

"You'll *have* to speak to Dad," he began practically.

"I will not!"

I was so frustrated! It was a situation I couldn't do one thing about. I didn't even know for sure what I would want to do about it, if I could do anything, but I did know that I wanted our dad to be *our dad*, not some woman's go-to-Austin-for-the-weekend boyfriend.

"Maybe . . ." Luke swallowed. "Maybe we're just jealous for Mama," he ended softly.

At that, Harry started to cry which made me so mad all over again that I burst out, "That's stupid. Mama's dead."

Which was the first time I had ever said it out loud. I knew it one hundred percent, all the way to my soul, no question, no looking away from it. But it somehow made it even truer, and harder, and uglier, to say it out loud.

I had barely calmed down when Katie and them got there to watch movies. And I didn't even get out *Rebecca*. I wasn't in the mood for a story about a man who remarries after his first wife dies. Also, for the first time I can think of, I didn't really take in what Katie had on or who she was currently mad at. My mind wasn't on the movies, or even on Katie.

I had decided what to do.

Chapter 12

Dad got back about four o'clock Sunday afternoon. He'd already taken her home. Harry and Johnny were all over him like nothing had happened. Luke was a little more withdrawn, but he wasn't rude.

I did not come out of my room, where I had gone when I heard Johnny boofing at the familiar car sound coming in the driveway. I have a nice little chair that had been Grandmother's. She said they'd called them boudoir chairs. It's a small armchair with a little footstool. I was in it, with my American literature book open in my lap. I was not reading it.

He tap-tapped and opened the door.

"Hi, Rose, I'm home. How'd it go?"

I did not open my mouth.

He came over to me and sat down on the little footstool. He took the book out of my hands.

I would not look at him.

"Rose? What's the matter?"

I did not open my mouth.

"Rose, what is it?"

The curtain was crooked at the edge of the sill. I needed to straighten the rod from the top again. I stared at it.

"Did you have a set-to with the boys while I was gone?"

The other end of the curtain seemed to be hanging fine. Must be that brace thing in the center that I needed to jiggle.

"Rose, you have a count of fifteen to look at me and tell me what's the matter," Dad said, and now his voice was getting very lawyerish. He had started out sweet.

Guts is a great thing. I've got 'em. But sometimes I don't have good sense about when to use them.

I looked him straight in the eye and said, "Mama wouldn't like you sleeping with that woman and neither do I."

He slapped me.

He had never done that before in my life. Nor had he ever in their lives slapped either one of the boys, to my certain knowledge, because they'd have told me if he had.

He didn't want to. He couldn't help himself. I know that, too, because by the time his hand had actually touched my face, he had almost got it stopped. It hurt like fire, but it wasn't bruising like it would have been if he hadn't tried so hard to put the brakes on. His face was red as a beet, and his eyes were so bright that they glistened.

I think my face must have been red, too, and not just from where he'd slapped me. My mouth flew open and I hit my bed howling and pulled the covers all the way over my head, curling up on my knees, shrieking, sobbing, howling. My nose was snotty, my hair was all undone and getting wet from the tears and I was shaking all over, crying with every inch of my body.

Suddenly the covers were yanked back. He was shaking, too, but his face wasn't red anymore and he was standing tall as a tree. I snatched at the covers, but he had not let go of them. I was this curled-up ball of miserable crying person, all uncovered.

He said, "Get undressed and get into the shower. Then put on your sweats and come into the living room. You have fifteen minutes till I come after you."

And he was gone.

I knew I'd bought the farm.

My eyes were swollen nearly shut when I sat down on the sofa about twelve minutes later. I'd kept on howling in the shower because it took a while to be able to quit. It was another one of those horrible hiccupping several-things-rolled-into-one cries. I cried because he had taken Miss Welman to Austin, I cried because I had kept my resolve to myself and said that awful thing to him, I cried because he had slapped me, I cried because I had done something so terrible that he couldn't keep himself from it, I cried because Mama was dead and our best dog was dead and we were not a real family like we used to be.

Luke and Harry were already assembled on the sofa, and Dad was standing by the mantel looking very much as if he were in court. The boys didn't look at me, nor did I look at them.

"Rose," he said when I sat down. I was looking straight at him, and my heart was pounding.

"Boys," he said. But they were already looking straight at him, too. Johnny was even quiet, lying down in the middle of the floor, wide awake.

"It is very hard in our circumstances to know where my privacy stops and your interests begin. I see now that I should have told you before the week-end what my plans were. I surprised you and upset you, and I am sorry for that.

"But you'll note that I said, 'should have *told* you.'

In spite of our deep, deep love and concern for one
another, it remains that you are the minors and I am
the adult. I will not, therefore, be asking you for
permission or confirmation for my personal plans."
It was Ben The Lawyer talking. "You know that I
would not ever knowingly hurt you. Luke?" He was
saying our names and looking into our eyes in the
very same way I'd seen him look into the eyes of
individual jury members.

"Yessir."

"However, there may be times when what I do
does hurt you, perhaps because you don't entirely
understand it or perhaps because you don't agree
with what I'm doing. Miss Welman and I met her
brother in Austin for dinner. He had flown there on
business, and she was naturally eager to see him. I
was pleased to be invited to go along and meet him,
so I suggested that we make a weekend of it. We had
dinner at the Driskill and enjoyed the piano bar after
dinner. We had breakfast at Cisco's this morning
and then showed her brother a little bit of Austin
before we left him to his paperwork and came home.
Harry?"

"Yessir."

"Now. My privacy, and Miss Welman's, begins
with whatever sleeping arrangements we made. Obviously I like her. Otherwise I wouldn't have been

interested in meeting her brother or spending a day and a half in her company. I would give many years of my own life if your mother were still with us, but she is not. I believe we all knew her well enough to be able to say safely that she would be heartsick if she thought we were not making any effort to get on with our own lives, even though she can't share them with us anymore. Rose?"

"Yessir."

I had not taken my eyes off him. My heart was full of love and tears.

"Sir?"

"Yes, Luke?"

"Are you going to marry Miss Welman?"

"I don't know, Luke." Dad sat down in the chair across from us. "I'm not ready to decide that yet, for myself, and of course, if I did decide to ask her, then there would be her own decision to be made. For now, I enjoy being with her."

"Will you tell us if you ask her?" Harry's voice was tiny. It made him seem like a very little boy. Rowdy funny Harry.

There was a long, long pause. Then Dad said, "I hope so. It seems like it would be fair to talk it over with you, doesn't it? But I can't say definitely what I would do about that, either," and suddenly he smiled, almost chuckled. "I only ever asked one girl to marry me, and that was long before you were born."

To my horror, I giggled. It was an okay thing to do. I was just astonished that it happened.

"Luke, why don't you and Harry walk over to Hunan's and get us some fried rice and moo goo gai pan," he said, getting up so he could get some money out of his pocket. "Unless there are more questions?"

"Let's take Johnny, and I can hold him outside while you go in and pick up the food." Harry sounded more like Harry now.

When they were out the door, Dad sat beside me on the sofa.

"Rose, I'm ashamed of myself that I hit you."

"It's okay," I said. I did not say that I'd had it coming, although I was beginning to feel that I had.

"However"—so *he* said it, sort of—"you were way out of line."

"Yessir."

"Since I acted badly, too, I'm going to consider that we're even. No more punishment other than how bad we both already feel about it. But I am going to extract a promise."

"Yessir?"

"Surely I don't even have to, but just in case, I'm going to: you will be gracious to and about Marie. In

all circumstances. No more precocious judgmental-
ism. Do you understand me?"

"Yessir."

Silence for a second. Then he hugged me.

"I love you, Rose."

He looked so sad when he said it that I knew he
must be thinking the very same thing I was thinking
in the shower: how awful that our family had come
to such a sorry pass as this. That I had to be made
to promise to be gracious to a friend of my father's!

That my father *had* a friend.

Girlfriend, I mean.

Chapter 13

It was only a few days later that I got home late from school and there they were in the kitchen, Miss Welman and Dad and about nine million sacks of groceries.

Of course, once again, Dad hadn't told anybody anything.

Miss Welman was unshucking the sacks and setting a bunch of salad fixings in the sink basket, and Dad said, "We're having the Grants and the Kregers over for supper, did I tell you that this morning?"

"Nope. Are the boys coming home?"

"Luke is. Harry's at the Dietzes' and will be here after a while."

"Okay. I'munna put some jeans on. Hello, Miss

Welman," said Dad's Gracious Daughter, heading for her room.

When I came back, they were cutting up a chicken and talking a mile a minute. Looked to me like they knew each other very well. I wished that Luke would get on home. They'd put a bunch of potatoes in the drainer. I took a deep breath and asked did they want me to peel them, which they said they did. So when Luke walked in, I was peeling and they were cutting and the salad veggies were washing and draining.

He said hi to everybody and went to let Johnny in because of course ol' John was leaping up nearly to the height of the glass doors to the porch, trying to get some attention and be part of things. As soon as he was inside, he herded us all up together at the sink and got a spanking for making teeth marks in the back of Miss Welman's shoe heel.

"Luke, can you please pull the salad?" she said.

That expression was a new one on me, although I knew you weren't supposed to cut lettuce because it will go brown where the knife has been. Luke caught on, though, and got right into the sink brigade, shaking the water from the veggies in the drainer and pulling the lettuce apart.

"Ben, I think you better go get some ice," she said, and boy, ol' Dad just dried his hands and took off.

"Rose, let's chop those potatoes up fairly small so they'll cook faster," she said, and boy, I hacked them into little bitty pieces. Luke had finished with the lettuce and was into the other veggies.

"Johnnydog likes avocado," he said.

Johnnydog was by then lying down about two feet away from us, smarting from his spanking and pretending to be a good dog.

"I've heard that some dogs do." She smiled. "In fact, I have seen some tidbits for dogs that have dried avocado as the base ingredient. See if he'll sit for a bite."

He did sit. Then Luke offered him another bite and he rolled over for it, without even being asked to.

We all laughed. It had a very normal feel. Dad walked in with the ice while we were still laughing and ol' John was back to pretending to be a good dog by lying still in the middle of the kitchen. As long as he can see where everybody is—thinking, I guess, that he has his herd under control—he is good. But of course when Dad came in, Johnny leaped up like he hadn't seen him in days and jumped all over and boofed and licked and chomped on Dad's wrists and heels.

Dad set the ice down and got the no-no can. That's a Dr. Pepper can, washed out, with pennies in it. We wrapped ours in fancy paper to make it pretty, but you don't have to. You do have to seal up the drinking hole with tape. When you tell the dog no, you rattle the can. It is loud and clangy and dogs don't like it. You can even throw it at their tail, but not at their head because it could hurt them.

Mostly, I don't throw ours because Johnny is so fast that you can't be sure where he's going to be by the time the can gets to where he was. Dad just said, "No," and shook it at him and he quit hopping around and sort of went "Huffff" and lay down again.

When the Grants and Kregers came a few minutes later, Miss Welman went to the door with Dad. She had the no-no can and went into action the minute Johnny jumped up. We were laughing and saying hi to the folks' friends. *They* were laughing and kidding about Johnny's "clothes"—his bandanna, you know. He has a whole bunch of them now and it's sort of his trademark.

I loved it that things seemed more normal around our house, but it made me feel . . . wistful. It's the same on the outside as it was when we had Mama. But inside, it . . . isn't. She is not my mama. And this puppy is not our best dog. I felt good and bad at the same time.

When everybody went home, except Miss Welman, she and Dad started cleaning stuff up, and I went in to help them. I didn't think about being Dad's Gracious Daughter or anything.

I just went in there, *normal*-ly, and they just kept on talking and handing each other or me dishes to load or put up or whatever. *Normal*-ly. Suddenly, I was very confused.

Chapter 14

A couple of days later, she called the house. I answered the phone.

"Rose? This is Marie Welman."

"Hi, Miss Welman. Dad's not here."

"Well, can you take a message for him? For all of you, really. I called the office first and his secretary took a note for him to call me back, but then I thought I'd just go ahead and call you." She almost sounded nervous. "Our school's Fun Night is Friday—maybe Harry told you. . . ."

"Yes, ma'am. He's going to be a Red Racer in that thing his room's doing."

"Oh, good. Well. I was thinking that maybe we could all go together. I will have to work with my room some, of course, and so will Harry with his, but we could eat together. I'd like you to be my guests."

"Ummm, okay, umm, that sounds nice. I'll check with Dad and ask him to call you." Rats. I hate it when I say "Umm." I guess I was a little nervous, too.

It suited Dad just fine for us all to go with Miss Welman to Fun Night. He acted like he was sort of impressed that she thought of it. I wasn't sure it was that much of a deal. After all, she knew we practically had to go anyway because of Harry.

We picked Miss Welman up and when we got to the school, she went to her room to get them started on where they were selling cotton candy. They had rented a machine and bought the sugar and colors and were making cone puffs of blue and pink cotton candy for fifty cents each. There were lots of parents helping, too.

Luke got some, and then we went on over to Harry's room's spot so he could get started with them on their project. They'd blocked off an area of the parking lot and had drawn a maze on it. Two kids were Red Racers—Harry and a little girl that I'd met at dog school with her wirehaired terrier—and four other kids were Green Growlers. You paid a quarter and Harry or Kilah would run around the maze while you told them which way to go to get away from the Growlers. They had flaps of green material that they had to flip over if they got caught and were supposed to pretend to disappear. It was real cute.

Miss Welman got our barbecue tickets as soon as the line formed, but we never did get any food.

"Mr. Marlin! Mr. Marlin!" Kilah, with her Red Racer shirt flying, was tearing through the line to Dad.

"Harry's hurt! He fell down, bad." She grabbed Dad's hand and took off zigging through the crowd the way she'd come, with Dad in tow and Luke hard on their heels.

"Leave your purse and Luke's things. I'll stay here with our stuff till you find out what happened," said Miss Welman, who slid out of the line immediately.

"I'll be right back," I yelled, beating feet.

There was quite a crowd around poor ol' Harry by the time I got over there. His face was all squeezed up like a rotten orange and nearly that color, too, with a little tear or two at the corners of his squinched-up eyes. But he wasn't making a sound. Dad was on his knees beside him, looking at his right arm. Luke was nowhere to be seen. Turned out he was looking for Dr. Gomez, who was there on the grounds somewhere.

But I could have told them Harry's arm was broken. Nobody's arm can bend like that if it's not.

"We can take him over in your car, Ben; he doesn't seem to be hurt anywhere else," Dr. Gomez said after she'd taken a good look at Harry.

"I'll go get the car." Dad got up and took off.

Luke and the doctor helped Harry up, Dr. Gomez holding Harry's arm just right. Everybody but me seemed to have completely forgotten Miss Welman.

"Luke, don't leave without me. I gotta go tell Miss Welman what happened."

The people who'd been in the crowd by Harry started milling around, getting back to whatever they'd been doing, telling each other what had happened and how much of it they'd seen. Kilah was the Most Important Witness, since she'd been in the big pileup, too, a Growler sandwich on the pavement. She said she'd heard Harry's bone snap.

About halfway back to the food area, I met Miss Welman coming to look for us. She had my purse and the flashlight Dad had brought for later on, and some paper sack thing that Luke had had.

"There's not going to be room in the car for all of us," she said. "You want to walk over to my place with me? We'll get my car and meet them at Emergency."

"I'll go with y'all. It's getting pretty dark for you to walk over there by yourselves," Luke said.

What a guy. I was about as scared of the dark as I would be of a baby kitten, but see how sweet Luke is? If I couldn't go in the car with Harry, he wouldn't go either.

Hospitals are so bright. Those light bright walls and white white tile floors. It was in this very building that we last saw Mama, but I didn't think of that till later. Cancer patients don't spend much time in emergency rooms, I guess. We'd never been in this wing before.

I was all sweaty and Luke's hair was standing on end, so I suppose mine was, too. Miss Welman looked a little rumpled up herself, but she was completely calm and just sort of took charge. I mean, when we walked in the door of all that bright whiteness, she stepped ahead of us and up to the desk. Had her arm around my waist and her hand on Luke's arm.

"We're with Harry Marlin," she said.

"Oh, yes," said the nurse. "Please wait in those green chairs. The doctor is with him now."

"Where's Dad?" Luke was looking around.

"Probably in there with them," Miss Welman whispered.

She got out some change. "Luke, there's a Coke machine down the hall, I think. Go get us something to drink."

"Harry's brave, huh?" I said. I felt like I might cry, for Pete's sake, and there was nothing on earth really wrong with him. She squeezed me.

"Yes, and so are you. Something like this is scary. It's not serious. We all know it isn't serious. But it's a shock, and it's worrisome."

The cold drinks were a real tonic. Her arm around me was nice. I think Mama must have hugged us quite a bit. At the time, I probably didn't even think about it.

Dad was smiling when he came around the corner. We all stood up and Luke handed Dad the rest of his cold drink. Dad took a big chug before he spoke.

"He's fine," he said. "He's mad, and he'll be hurting pretty badly later on tonight when the shot wears off. But it was a nice clean break, about two inches above his wrist, and they think they have a good set on it. I'll go get the car, and you bring him out, okay? They are putting him in a wheelchair in case he's a little woozy."

A nurse was pushing Harry's chair, and Dr. Gomez and another doctor were walking alongside. Everybody seemed cheerful, and Harry looked pretty stuck on himself, riding along in that fancy wheelchair with two doctors flanking him. Miss Welman kissed him and he smiled all over himself.

We put him in the front seat with Dad, who said, "Marie, can you take Dr. Gomez back to the school—her car's there—and then maybe come over?"

"Sure. I'll help my room clean up their booth, and then—"

"I'll go with you," Luke said. "Rose, you can help Dad get Harry into bed."

Miss Welman and Luke and the doctor went on, and we drove off very slowly, so as not to jostle Harry's arm.

"Where's ol' Kilah?" Harry asked all of a sudden.

"She's still at school, I guess. She's fine."

"Well. No more soccer this year."

"Yeah. But it wasn't anybody's fault, Harry."

"I know. But our soccer team was creamin' 'em."

"Yeah."

Chapter 15

Johnny was jumping up and down and hollering at the glass doors when we got home, but I didn't open the doors because I figured we better get Harry settled before the Jumper came in. Dad tended to that, and I went to the kitchen to fix a pitcher of tea. Johnny was really yowling and he kept shaking his ears. They were still big satellite-dish ears—he hadn't grown into them yet—and when he shook them like that, they made a loud flap-flap sound.

I took the tea into the boys' room. Dad was sitting on Harry's bed and we all took a glass and kind of grinned at each other. Harry's eyes kept closing, but he drank quite a bit of his tea.

"Is that this cast, or is there a skunk outside?" he

said in a blurry voice. Come to think of it, I'd been faintly smelling something, too.

"It's a skunk in the neighborhood," Dad laughed. "Your cast doesn't smell—yet."

"That's why Johnny's raising such a fit." Harry handed Dad his glass and went down for the count.

We heard the back door open, and then the worst yell we'd heard in the entire crisis.

"Oh NOOOOO!" Luke was bellering, slamming the glass door in the midst of a blast of ki-yi-yiis. Dad and I rushed into the living room, and there sat Miss Welman in the little rust chair, laughing so hard that she wasn't making any noise and tears were rolling down her cheeks. Luke, breathing hard, was standing with his back against the door, and ol' Johnny was *sitting* on the outside of it, whimpering, ears down, tail down, eyes wild.

"Come on, Dad, let's go get the tomato juice," Luke said tersely. He obviously didn't think it was very funny, but Dad started laughing, too.

I opened the glass door a crack, and I'm telling you, have you ever smelled anything that was so strong you thought you could hear it? It was *loud*, it smelled so strong. I mean, like being inside a drum with somebody beating on it. I never knew your senses could get mixed up like that. Johnny and that skunk had sure enough met each other.

Dad and Luke ran up to the 7-Eleven to get some of those big twenty-ounce cans of tomato juice and they bathed him with it in an old plastic laundry tub. In the yard, of course. Johnny cried the whole time, but he didn't try very hard to get away from them. I guess he realized he needed that bath.

Luke had put the leash on him and was holding him, while Dad poured the tomato juice over him over and over again. They threw the dirty juice in the alley and washed down the tub, and then Miss Welman and I took over for the soaping part.

"Here, Miss Welman, tie this towel over your dress," I said, handing her one of the two I'd pulled out of the drawer. We already had our shoes off, and I wasn't very dressed up to start with. We had my Swiss Formula good-smelling shampoo, because I'd decided having Johnny smell nice was worth the sacrifice. His doggy stuff smells like medicine.

"I'll hold him, and you scrub," Miss Welman said.

Luke and Dad handed him over and went on in the house to get cleaned up.

He lathered up great which meant they'd got the skunk oil off, I guess, and really, we could hardly smell it on him, but it did still sort of hang in the air. Miss Welman held onto him and talked gently to him the whole time. We had his collar down in the soapy water with him, but we wound up having to throw it and that day's bandanna away.

"Miss Welman," I said, rubbing the shampoo in waves and circles on ol' John, "I had a good time tonight. Thank you for inviting us to Fun Night."

That didn't sound quite right, since Harry had broken his arm, but what I wanted to say was that I was sorry I'd been such a brat about her. And I couldn't say that because as far as I knew she didn't know I had been. Unless she had just been able to sense it. Which I certainly hoped she had not.

She just smiled and kept her vise-grip on Johnny. I reached over for the hose and started giving him the first rinse. If she had known that I'd been mean-spirited about her, maybe that smile meant that I was forgiven. I almost felt like crying.

Right away, when that prickly feeling started, I thought about poor ol' Harry.

"Poor ol' Harry," I said out loud.

"He'll be fine, honey. It's too bad, but little boys play rough and sometimes they get hurt," she said, still in that creamy gentle voice she was using to keep Johnny calm.

"I hope you'll come over and see him," I blurted, and dove back into the second shampooing wave.

"Why, thank you. Yes, I will. But he'll be back in school by Monday, I promise," she said.

I just about had all the second soaping off Johnny
when he jerked loose from us and set off running in
circles around the yard, shaking water and slinging
the last dollops of soap all over us. He ran and ran
and ran and shook and flung and slung, and we sat
down in the grass, our clothes pretty well ruined,
laughing at him.

Chapter 16

The next day I had to take Johnny out for his walk by myself, on account of Harry's arm and Luke's having a term paper. We were heeling, staying, downing, and heeling like crazy because dog-school finals were coming up. And when we turned the corner into Comanche Street, here came a couple walking their dog. The guy was a real cowboy type, hat and all, and even the woman had on real jeans, not the designer kind. But the big deal was that their dog was a blue heeler, too!

It was a short squatty one like First Johnny, not a tall skinny one like Now Johnny, and its tail had been docked. Lots of times, in this part of the country, they dock heelers' gorgeous fluffy foxy tails, especially if they are really working dogs, because of the heavy brush and also the coyotes. Coyotes chase dogs, I suppose you know, and heelers will chase them back and they are nearly as fast, but not quite. It's been known for a coyote to bite off a heeler's tail when he's got the dog on the run. Anyway, so this dog had no tail but otherwise looked *exactly* like First Johnny. Seeing it first head on, so that I couldn't tell immediately about no tail, was pretty startling.

The other people seemed surprised, too, to see another blue heeler. The man said, "Well, g'd evenin'. You got yourself a fine heeler there. Not many people got 'em in town."

He clearly thought this was odd, even though there he stood with one himself.

"This is a house dog and he's our second one," I said, proud, frankly, to have such a tough dog. "We had a shorter one, exactly like yours, for fourteen years until he died. Then we got this one. But our first one didn't have his tail cut off either."

"Missy was born on my dad's ranch," the woman said, "and their tails were docked as pups because . . ." and then she told all that stuff I just told you about brush and coyotes. I did not, of course, expose that I already knew it, since that wouldn't have been polite, and since it makes people happy to think they've told you something new or taught you something. And besides I didn't want to act like a smarty-pants.

"Missy's eleven," the woman said. "I hope she'll live as long as your other one did."

"Well, she will, in town," the man said to her. "Vet told me the reason their life span is only supposed to be nine years is that most of 'em live in the outdoors and work. Harder lives. More dangers to 'em."

"I won't be getting another one," the woman said. "I couldn't stand it."

"Oh no!" I said. Best way to describe it would be to say that I heard those words burst out of me, because I sure didn't know that I was going to say it. "No! You love this dog, and you'll love another one like her! You shouldn't let loving one thing keep you from loving another thing! Things die! You can't help it!"

My head was whirling and I'd let go of Johnny's lead. I was glad, though, because when I realized what I'd said, I needed to bend down and pick it up so that they couldn't see I was about to cry. They didn't see, and the woman just said, "Well, maybe." She looked off down the street. "I used to have cats as a kid, but I've never had another one since my favorite died. I miss cats."

We said it was a pretty evening, and hadn't the sunsets been nice, and then went on with our walks in opposite directions, like we had been going before we met each other.

But I was nearly stumbling on the way home and tingling all over. I kept my eyes opened very wide so that the tears would have more room and wouldn't spill out. I was thinking about Miss Welman and Dad and the night they had the Grants and the Kregers over to dinner and how normal it had felt. And how nice Miss Welman was about helping bathe skunky Johnny. And how much Harry liked her. And how it wasn't the same as our family used to be, but it was very nice. . . . I thought, Good grief, that's *right* what I said to those people, and I didn't even know it myself till I said it. I *have* got to where I love Now Johnny as much as I did First Johnny, just about, and it doesn't take away one bit from how much I loved *him* and what a great dog he was, the very best ever, no question about it. It's *different* with this Johnny. It's not "better" or "more" or "less." Just different.

It's probably the same way with loving people. Maybe you aren't supposed to compare the way you feel about human beings with the way you feel about animals. But it's the *idea*, the thinking behind the way you're feeling. You *can* compare that.

Chapter 17

Harry was pretty much okay by that evening. He tried to string out the sympathy till Tuesday before he went back to school, but it didn't work.

The strangest thing, though. We didn't see Miss Welman or hear Dad mention her at all that whole week or the next weekend. Of course we were very busy because dog-school finals were coming up. We were tripling up on Johnny's homework. Each of the three of us, even Harry in his cast, was taking him through his lessons after school every day.

I think Johnny understood about the cast. He was always good and gentle with Harry, never pulled any of his silly jumping-around-on-the-leash nonsense. With Luke and me, when we'd first put the leash on him, he'd act like he thought *he* was leading the walk. He'd take the leash in his mouth about a foot from his collar and trot like a circus pony, pretending to be boss. But he didn't do that with Harry while he had the cast on.

Saturday I began to really kind of miss Miss Welman, and that night when Dad stayed home, I started to mention it, but I didn't know if he'd get mad and say that it was grown-ups' business. I didn't want to get in trouble like I did after they went to Austin.

Dad stayed home the next day, too. He was moping around, in fact. I began to wonder if maybe I *should* say something.

Late in the afternoon, I gathered up the boys in their room.

"We need a Council," I said, "on the topic 'Is Miss Welman mad at Dad?' "

They reacted characteristically. Harry picked it up at once. "Yeah. What's the deal? I miss her."

Luke was ponderous and more logical. "How would *we* know, Rose? And it's none of our business, anyway. You know what Dad'd say. Grown-up business. Not ours."

I pounced on that. It was the phrase that jelled what had been ringing around in my head.

"Not entirely," I said. "Look, help me with this. I know I got out of line about that Austin thing. A lot of that really *was* their business, not ours. But, listen, I think maybe it's all our business now. I mean, we know her now. We—" I gulped, disgusted to discover that I was feeling through this so hard that I was almost teary. "We—like—her. Don't we?"

"Yeah! She's *baaad!*" Harry hollered.

"Shhh." Luke hooked his thumb at the door. Dad was out there somewhere in the rest of the house or in the yard, maybe.

"Yeah," he finally said, more slowly than Harry. "I like her, too, but I'm still not sure that who Dad dates . . ." That *word* . . . Luke trailed off.

"Well, look. This is the part I want you to help me think through. I think you're right, and early on Dad was right, that who he *dates* is not exactly up to us to say. I mean, if she's not a criminal or some-thing. I mean, like when we start dating ourselves, he would make it his business that we not date some sleazebag, but if it was an okay person, nothing wrong with them, but he just didn't personally care too much for them, he wouldn't be supposed to stop us from just having a date with them. *But* if we started really being with one person a *lot*, don't you think Dad would think he should know about it?"

"Oh, sure." Luke jumped right on that one. "He'd be telling us right away, then, what he thought of the person and we'd probably figure he had a right to, even if we didn't like what he said."

"Okay. Now. This is what I'm talking about. He has been, more or less, in whatever term their crowd would use for it, *going* with Miss Welman for several months."

"Since right after school started," Harry said. "But me and Luke met her before you did. Me and Luke met her at the Kregers'."

"Luke and I," said Luke.

"I know it," said Harry.

"So," I went on, "now it *is* our business, too. I mean, if he's really *going* with her, this woman could be going to be . . . our mother."

"No. She could not be. Nobody else can ever be that." Luke sounded suddenly very adult. "Not our *mother*. But she *could* be one of our dearest friends. She *could* be Dad's wife, and we could be . . . close . . . to . . . her . . ."

"And love her," Harry chimed in.

"And let her be . . . family," I said slowly.

"Yes," he said, "we could. If Dad did."

"We could love her, all on her own," I went on. "Not like Mama, not the same. Different. But good. Maybe even just as much, but in a different way."

"And she could come to PTO and represent me," Harry crowed. "She could be my mother for the PTO, couldn't she?"

Luke and I looked at each other.

"I guess that would be okay," I said hesitantly. "But, see, he hasn't even called her, as far as we know, all this week. I think we need to have a Council with him. Will you guys back me up if I do the talking?"

"We are going to feel stupid if she's just been out of town, or if he did something awful to her and she told him to stay out of her face," Luke said, and now he grinned. Or if Dad's decided he doesn't like her, I thought, horrified.

"So will you back me up?" I hammered on. "I'll beat the stuffing out of you if you let me get him in here and then act like you don't know what I'm talking about."

"We'll back you up!" Harry hollered. "Go for it! We're your damn brothers, aren't we?"

"Harry, don't cuss. Miss Welman doesn't like it," I said primly.

My heart was about to thump out of my T-shirt, but I went to look for Dad. He was just sitting on the porch, not reading the paper or anything, sort of absently patting ol' John, who, of course, jumped up and began to bounce around when I opened the door.

Chapter 18

"**D**ad. Council." Boy, this was already hard!

"What?"

"Council. We want to have a family council."

"Oh. Sure." He came on in and started to sit down in the living room. I happened to all of a sudden remember something I'd heard on TV about negotiating, and how if you are the one asking for something, you should get the other person to come into your own territory. So I said, "Let's go in the boys' room."

He sat down on the chair at Luke's desk. Luke and Harry were still sitting on their beds, Luke straight as a post, Harry sprawled around. Johnny boofed at the glass door. We'd closed it more or less in his face.

I sat on the little wooden trunk that Luke had made in Scouts and kept at the foot of his bed.

"Dad," I said, breaking the electric silence, "we noticed you didn't see Miss Welman this week. For about ten days, in fact," I sounded squeaky to myself.

"That's right," he said.

Boy, he wasn't planning to help me.

"Did . . . did y'all have a fight?" I sure did *hope* I wasn't squeaking.

"No."

"Well . . . ummm . . . do you still like her?"

"Is this Council about Miss Welman and me? I thought I'd made myself clear that—"

"Wait, Dad," Luke interrupted. God love ol' Luke. He was for sure going to help me! I might have cratered if he hadn't come on in.

"We know you and your . . . uh . . . friends . . . are mostly just your business by yourself. And themselves, too, I mean, but see, we like Miss Welman. . . ," Luke said with those little count-of-seven pauses.

"Yeah, we do, and we thought you did." Ol' Harry couldn't wait for the pauses.

"Dad"—I had it together better now—"we feel like you let us be a part of you and Miss Welman being friends, and we feel like that affects all of us, so we think if things are changed between you, or something, you ought to tell us."

"She was here last weekend when I broke my arm and everything!" Harry hollered.

For a second, I felt about seven years old myself and wanted to yowl, "Yeah, and she helped me bathe the tomato juice off ol' Johnny!" but I didn't. I swallowed and said, "We don't want to be nosy, and we know you are an adult and we aren't. But we are, except for Grandmother who doesn't live here, the only family each other has. So we think when something important is going on with you, you ought to let us in on it. We would let *you* in on *our* stuff."

Dad was looking at the floor. And then at his hands. When he looked up, he looked right into my eyes and I swear his were shiny. He said—after about a count of seven!—"You make a good point. Objection sustained." And he sighed. Well, no. It was more like he'd been holding his breath and then he let it out. He said, "I was becoming very fond of Marie. Miss Welman. I liked her as a person. I liked her with my other friends. I liked the way she was herself, not different, but sincerely herself, and open, with you kids. She . . . is . . . a good woman. I thought maybe . . ."

And he couldn't go on! Our *dad* couldn't go on

with his sentence! My heart turned completely over and quit slamming. It settled in like a real heart, and I felt—oboy, you are going to think this is really crazy—I felt a premonition of what I might be like when I am grown. I felt a settling-in, a solidness, and it was firm, but it was soft. I said, "Well, Dad, don't you still like her?"

He was looking right at me. Then he looked right at Luke, who'd had his head down but lifted it then and met Dad's eyes straight on. Then Dad looked at Harry, who was wiggling and bouncing, a little bit like Johnny, but who was not blinking.

"Yes. I do. But it's . . . soon. It's pretty . . . *soon.* I thought maybe I shouldn't be on the edge of making a permanent choice so . . . soon. It has to be the right choice, not just for me, but for all of us. . . ."

I said—oh, where did it come from out of me to say this?—"That's so wonderful. Oh, dad, that's so wonderful! But, see, we want the best for you, too. And we know that she isn't ever going to be Mama. She isn't supposed to be Mama. She is supposed to be her own self. See, if you'd just *talk* to us . . ." But that tone of voice sounded like a whiny-baby to me, and I knew I had to keep strong and say this right.

Carefully, I started again. "See, maybe this is going to sound silly, but it isn't silly. I just don't know a better way to say it. See, it's sort of like there will never be another First Johnny. No matter what, or where, or who, or anything, he was the very best dog in the world. But he's gone, and now we have *this* Johnny, and he's different, and he's too feisty, but he's himself and he loves us and we love him and he makes us laugh and he's going to be the by-golly star at dog-school finals and he's *ours* and things change, things get lost, but other things come, and we like the new things, too, and we have to change our own selves, and Miss Welman isn't Mama, but we can't have Mama and we like Miss Welman . . . ," and I realized that even though I was speaking so slowly, I was crying again. Good grief, I have cried more in the past two years than I ever did in my whole life before that. But this time it felt different somehow.

Then Harry, silly ol' Hollering Harry hollered, "Daddy, I want Miss Welman to come over and sign my cast! Wouldn't you even let her just come over and sign my cast?"

And Dad said, "Yes, I think maybe I could ask her to come over and sign your cast."

He took a very deep breath. He blinked, and his eyes weren't shiny anymore. He said, "I'll tell you what: this was a good Council. It's the best we've ever had, because I have learned so much. I want you to know that I see now that I can't keep important family business from you just because you are so much younger than I am. And I see that now you can accept the fact that there are some pieces of my life that I can't share equally with you because you are not quite mature enough yet to sort them out correctly. But now that we have all these important facts established, we won't ever get so tangled up again.

"I'll call Marie. What she and I work out will be up to us. After all, she is coming into this whole equation from her own standpoint. But I'll tell her we are speaking to her through me as a whole family. And I'll tell you what she has to say."

Finally, I understood the difference between being entirely grown-up and being just a decent distance along the way. And I knew that the reason Dad had finally been able to open up to us and to help me understand that, and to help Luke and Harry understand it, too, was that *I* had had the courage to broach the subject directly, sincerely, totally, in a very adult family council.

Pride is a sin. It goeth before a fall. Mama used to say that. But you do for sure have to know it when you do a good thing.

"Boys, let's play like this Council is over," I said.

"It *is* over," Luke said.

"Yeah, but I mean let's don't sit here and wait to

hear what he says to Miss Welman, or if he even calls her, or if she even answers. Let's give him his grown-man privacy, and just get on with our own—I mean, let's, uh, just—"

"I know! Let's not push it!" Harry rolled back over on himself in his bed, like a somersault. "Maybe if we can just shut up, we'll get me a PTO mom!"

Before I could get up to do it myself, Luke had ambled out through the hall and let Johnny in.

So when Dad came out of his room, we were all three wallowing around on the living room floor with silly ol' Johnny. Dad was smiling from ear to ear, and he said, "What do you want to cook tomorrow night? Miss Welman is coming to dinner."

Chapter 19

Well, you know the rest, I guess.

There were two best parts, though, that I just have to mention before I stop. The first was dog-school finals.

By then, Dad and Marie—we all call her Marie now, but sometimes Harry slips and calls her Mom—by then, Dad and Marie were engaged. They'd told the Grants and the Kregers, and people were entertaining for them, and everybody was all excited. Everybody kept saying, "And how do the children like her?"

And we were saying, "We like her fine," and rolling our eyes privately because, hey, we had practically planned the whole thing when you come right down to it. But we let Dad have the credit.

Anyway, dog-school finals was kind of our coming-out party as a family. We all dressed up slick, but in appropriate gear for curb-sitting, and ol' Luke put Baby John through his paces.

The Majorette was there, looking like she'd been bathed in Lemon Clorox and smelling like she'd been doused with Giorgio. The rottweilers were there with brand-new red leather collars, over their required dog-school chain ones, of course. Johnny had been scrubbed and brushed till he looked like new pewter. He had on a bright blue cowboy bandanna.

He was pretty excited, but he went right through every command in line with his classmates, not jumping up on a soul, not even boofing, not offering to bite any dogs or run out of line. The very last thing was a long sit-stay: put your dog on sit and stay, turn around, walk to the end of the lead, and count to sixty. I'm sure it's longer for older dogs, or maybe something harder, but you remember that this was puppy pre-K.

We weren't worried about this command at all for Johnny, because it was so much like Monkey in the Middle and he'd been such a star at that, so by the time he got to this point in his test, we were all just sitting there grinning and figuring we were home free and the family of a graduate dog.

Well, don't count your chickens.

He sat there about five seconds, and then he began that little baby-talk whine he does when he wants somebody to pay attention to him. He just kind of goes, "Uh, uh," very softly in a high pitch. I could see Luke's ears getting red, but he didn't turn around. Johnny got a little louder. We quit grinning.

Then Johnny went to a down, and I thought, Rats, it's over. He broke his sit-stay; they may not pass him even though he did the rest of it so well. And about that time, he let out a pretty good little baby-talk howl, and began to roll over!

He rolled over three times and had his leash all wound around him, and the watchers started laughing, and poor red-faced Luke turned around, and the minute Luke turned to face him, ol' Johnny sat back up, all innocence, in perfect sit-stay—with his leash wrapped three times around his silly spoiled little body and looped over one ear. The whole crowd applauded and even the teacher laughed. She passed him.

The other best part that happened was the wedding. Grandmother went with us to Indiana for it in June and both "sides" got along great. Turns out, besides a brother, which you know about from the Austin Episode, Marie has these neat parents, and a sister who has two boys, one on either side of my very own age. So now we have cousins and aunts and uncles and more grandparents.

Harry and our new boy cousins seated people in the church, and Luke was best man. Best *man!* You should have seen him. But guess what: I was maid of honor. Marie's sister and I were her attendants and I had the most luscious pale green dress with little tiny roses on it. They got married in the late afternoon, with the church doors open, so that inside it smelled like grass and flowers because there were all kinds of honeysuckle blooming in the yard. . . . I almost said *we* got married in the late afternoon.

It really did feel like we were all getting married to each other, somehow.

Johnny didn't go, of course. But then he *is* a dog, not a human being.